MR. STRONG
and the flood

Original concept by Roger Hargreaves
Illustrated and written by Adam Hargreaves

MR. MEN **LITTLE MISS**

MR. MEN™ LITTLE MISS™ © THOIP (a Sanrio company)

Mr. Strong and the flood © 1998 THOIP (a Sanrio company)
Printed and published under licence from Price Stern Sloan, Inc., Los Angeles.
This edition published in 2012 by Dean, an imprint of Egmont UK Limited,
239 Kensington High Street, London W8 6SA

ISBN 978 0 6035 6773 5
54184/1
Printed in China

Mr Strong is unbelievably strong.

So strong that sometimes he forgets his own strength.

Like the other day.

It was raining.

So Mr Strong pulled on his wellington boots. But he pulled too hard and his foot went right through the bottom of his boot!

Then he went out through his front door and opened his umbrella.

But he pushed too hard and turned the umbrella inside out!

So he tried to go back inside to get another umbrella (Mr Strong gets through a lot of umbrellas) but when he turned the doorknob it came off in his hand.

Poor Mr Strong was not having a good day.

Fortunately, when you are as strong as Mr Strong you don't need a door to get inside your house.

Do you know what he did?

He picked up the corner of his house and slipped in under the wall!

Once he had fetched a new umbrella and opened it (very carefully this time) and opened his door (very carefully) he set off for his walk.

Now, as you might remember, I mentioned that it was raining.

What I did not tell you was that it had been raining for days and days and days.

Nearly a whole week.

Non-stop!

The river in the valley below Mr Strong's house had burst its banks and was flooding the meadows.

Mr Strong walked down the lane beneath the dripping trees.

It was not long before he met a very worried looking Farmer Fields.

"Good morning," said Mr Strong. "What's the matter?"

"It's my sheep," said Farmer Fields. "They're stuck in the meadow surrounded by water. I can't get them out!"

"Let's go and see," said Mr Strong. "I might be able to help."

Poor Farmer Fields' sheep were indeed in trouble.

And the bit of dry land left for them to stand on was getting smaller by the minute as the flood water rose higher.

Mr Strong waded out to the little island in the middle of the meadow and then waded back carrying two sheep above his head.

"Oh, well done," said Farmer Fields. "The only problem is that there are ninety-eight sheep left out there and we'll run out of time before you've carried them all across!"

"Mmmm," said Mr Strong. "I fear you may be right, but I think I have an idea. Do you mind if I borrow your barn?"

Farmer Fields smiled.

And you are probably smiling if you have read the other story about Mr Strong.

But for those of you who have not read that Mr Strong story, I'll tell you what he did.

He picked up the barn (that's right, a whole barn!) and carried it across to the sheep.

Then he lifted all the sheep into the barn.

Counting them carefully as he did, so as not to leave any behind.

And then he picked up the barn with all ninety-eight sheep inside, and waded back to Farmer Fields.

"Oh, thank you," said Farmer Fields, once all his sheep were safely in the field at the top of the hill.

"Barns are very handy things to have lying around," chuckled Mr Strong, and went home.

That evening Mr Strong ate an enormous plate full of fried eggs and went to bed early ...

... and fell fast ASHEEP! HA! HA!